A BOY, A DOG
and A FROG

by Mercer Mayer

To Ann

Lots of Love from

glynis b x b x

COLLINS St James's Place London

To my family,
Marianna and Samantha

First published in Great Britain 1974
© Mercer Mayer 1967
ISBN 0 00 195071-1
Made and Printed in Great Britain by
William Collins Sons & Co Ltd Glasgow